This igloo book belongs to:

....

igloobooks

Published in 2017
by Igloo Books Ltd
Cottage Farm
Sywell
NN6 0BJ
www.igloobooks.com

Illustrated by Dubravka Kolanovic
Original story by Jeannie Hund
Rewritten by Melanie Joyce

Cover designed by Nicholas Gage and Jason Shortland
Interiors designed by Jason Shortland
Edited by Hannah Cather

LEO002 0517
2 4 6 8 10 9 7 5 3 1
ISBN 978-1-78670-452-8

Printed and manufactured in China

I Love You So Much

igloobooks

I love you so much, little one.
You mean the whole world to me.

When I'm with you, there's
nowhere else I'd rather be.

I love it in the morning,
when you first see the sun.

You jump up and say,
"Let's play and have fun!"

I love our walks in the woods,
when we chatter away.

And how excited you get
when you hear music play.

You love to sit by the water
and watch the birds glide.

I put my arm around you
as you cuddle up by my side.

We love to lay down and
look at the stars at night.
I hold you and we giggle
under their twinkly light.

Everyone is tired as they
go home to their beds.
It's so cute when you say,
"Goodnight, sleepyheads!"

At bedtime, I say, "Snuggle up like this."
I stroke your head and give you a kiss.
I cherish all of our time together.
I love you so much. I'll love you forever.